THE CANYON

Dyer Wilk

Twisted
PUBLISHING

Dedication
For you.

A special thanks goes to John McIlveen for his sharp eye, and for noticing the little things I missed; to Michael Smith for providing me with a heavy book on the plants of Arizona, when Google searches just weren't working out for me; to Linda Angel for encouraging me to pursue this project even as it grew much larger than I intended; and to Chad Eagleton for being a sounding board on all things fiction and non-fiction. They made this book possible when lack of sleep and a heavy workload nearly kept it from happening.

Twisted Publishing is an imprint of Haverhill House Publishing

For more information, address:
Haverhill House Publishing
643 E Broadway
Haverhill MA 01830-2420
www.haverhillhouse.com

The world was thunder and pain and choking dust, and then darkness.

Some time later, a minute or a year, he felt daylight on his face and opened his eyes to the blinding sun. It beat down on his sprawled-out body as it always had, hot and unforgiving.

Gordon pulled himself up from the hard earth, his bones aching deep from the fall and his head full of hurt. He rubbed his face, and felt the dust bring stinging tears. He tried to blink them away, raking a soiled sleeve across his cheeks, but it did little good. He cried and cursed and coughed, and tried to walk to a spot where the air was fresh. But the dust was everywhere.

Somewhere close by he heard feet crunching on gravel.

Through the swimming distortion of tears and the pall of dust, he saw a man walking away from him.

"Over here," he called.

The man stopped and turned, trying to find him.

"Who is that?" the man asked.

He knew the voice, but his head was pounding too hard to determine which one exactly.

"It's me," he coughed in reply. "Gordon."

"You hurt?"

Gordon considered the question carefully, trying to measure the pain he felt against the worst kind of pain he could remember.

A clear answer didn't come.

"Can't say for sure," he said. "Not bad as far as I can tell."

"Wait right there."

Gordon waited. He still wasn't sure who he was talking to.

He watched as the man drifted further away, deeper into the blur of gray and brown.

"Hey, wait!" he called after him. "I'm over here."

A voice called back, faint. "I know that. Hold on a second. I need to check on..."

Gordon took half-a-dozen steps, trying to chase the fading words.

"You need to check on *what?*"

He stopped and listened closely.

The sound that came back was a whisper, maybe not even a voice at all. It could have been a faint breeze.

In the same moment, he felt the itching hot dust thin out around him and cooler air kiss his sweat-drenched skin.

For the first time since the fall, he could see where he was standing. The ground at his feet was nearly flat, but a few yards to his right it climbed sharply into a scree of chipped sandstone and gray-green shale. His eyes traced the length of the slope, and spotted a horse lying twisted midway up. He didn't need to come any closer to know that its neck had been snapped, just as he didn't need to inspect the saddlebags to see that the horse had belonged to him. He'd ridden that Appaloosa mare for the last eight months.

Sadness prodded him, but he quickly buried it within himself, refusing to let it fully blossom into regret. There was nothing he could do.

Gordon batted the dust away from his face with the flat of his hand, and walked toward the scree, stopping as his boots touched the incline of broken stones. Through the thin chalky haze, he saw the canyon walls towering high above him, marked three-quarters of the way up by a jagged scar of eroded dirt and rock where the trail had been only minutes before.

It must have been eighty feet up. Maybe a hundred.

He could hardly believe it.

A man had no right surviving a fall like that.

But he had.

He and whoever it was he'd seen loitering in the dust.

For the first time, since he'd come to, he wondered just how many of them had survived. When the trail had given way and become a surge of falling rock, there had been six of them.

No.

Not six.

Five.

Five because Tom hadn't been with them.

Gordon turned away from the scree and knelt down to sit. He closed his eyes and ran his fingers over his temples, trying to work the ache out of his head.

Less than a minute later, he heard the scream.

Gordon opened his eyes and sprang to his feet. The indeterminate pain that he felt everywhere became a sharp needling in the back of his neck.

In the distance, the cry echoed off the canyon walls. "I can see the bone!"

The words repeated, over and over, full of pain and desperation.

He ran toward the voice, knowing who it belonged to before he could put a name to it.

As he crested a rise of cracked mud and sand, he saw Jimmy Jones staggering away from a dead horse lying a few yards from the base of the cliff. His left arm hung at his side, dripping red.

"Kid!" Gordon shouted.

Jimmy looked up at him, relief and agony bringing him to the verge of crying.

He hurried toward Gordon, and stumbled on a rock, going down on one knee. He tried to stand again and quickly gave up, choosing to sit instead, gripping the wounded limb tightly.

The tears trickled down his dusty face, forming drops of mud on his chin. "Feels like my arm's on fire."

"Hold on, kid. You wait right there."

Gordon slowly made his way down the steep embankment, choosing his steps carefully on the loose gravel. As he neared the bottom, Bill Webb appeared from nowhere, running over the uneven ground in a jackrabbit sprint. He crouched beside Jimmy and began tending to the arm before he could say a word to him.

The kid squeezed his eyes shut, bellowing at the slightest touch. "I'm gonna lose my arm. For Jesus's sake, they're gonna cut it off. I know they will."

"You just hush now," Bill said. "You're gonna be all right. It's just broke. Seen far worse than this during the war."

Bill was gentle with him, treating him more like a boy of five than a man of nineteen. He began to wrap the arm in a length of torn shirt, but made an effort not to touch the wound or the bone protruding from it.

Gordon turned away. He was starting to feel numb.

"Either of you seen Frank?"

Bill shook his head. "Not as yet. Seen Sam though. He's just over a ways. Got his leg caught in a stirrup, but he can still walk. He's getting the saddlebags off his horse."

"His mount alive?"

"No. And I can't say mine met with a kinder fate either. Your constitution unsullied, Gordon? You don't look too good."

"The fall knocked me out cold. But I'm all right, far as I can tell. "

"Thank the good Lord above for that. Think I'm about the same as you. Came to lying face down in the dirt, but if anything is broke, it hasn't hindered me yet. Did you see Tom?"

Gordon inhaled sharply, the deep ache in his head growing stronger until he could hear the blood pounding in his ears.

He could see Tom Talbert clearly, riding like hell along the top of the canyon with the rest of them, the faint report of rifles crackling from behind as the posse closed in.

He saw Tom, loosely gripping the reigns of his horse, turning to smile at him, as if he was enjoying this, as if nothing scared him at all.

He saw that smile go flat.

He saw the hole in his chest.

It had only been a moment, but it had been long enough.

He'd seen the look on Tom's face as he fell from his horse. The sound of the shot had come later. Delayed by the distance. By the time he'd heard it, Tom had already gone over the edge of the canyon and disappeared.

Gordon pulled a handkerchief out of his pocket and wiped his eyes. "Yeah, I saw him."

"Damn shame, going like that, if you ask me, but there are worse ways. Once knew a man out of Missouri...name of Seaton, I think...He was riding through a stand of oaks and didn't see this low branch. Sharp end went and stuck him right through the —"

"Are you almost finished?"

"Oh yeah. The kid's gonna be rolling his own cigarettes in no time. You want one before then, Jimmy, don't you hesitate to ask me."

Jimmy nodded, his face slicked with sweat.

"Still gonna have to set the bone though," Bill said. "You might want to bite down on a stick for this part."

A gruff, baritone voice replied from up on the hill behind them: "He'd be better off biting a Peyote button. It dulls the pain some."

Gordon looked up and saw a tall bull of a man with a rifle strapped to his back descending the slope, casually working the creases out of a dusty *Boss of the Plains* hat with his thick fingers.

"You hurt, Frank?" Gordon asked.

Frank cracked a worn smile. "Only my feelings on account of that five dollars you still owe me."

"I'll have to get around to paying you back. How about your bones though? Anything broken?"

"Busted my ribs up some. I'll live. Kid looks like he's destined for the saw though."

Jimmy's eyes filled with panic. He looked at Bill as if every reassurance up to that point had been a lie.

Bill looked at Frank, scowling. "Now why in the Lord's name did you have to go and put such a notion into the boy's head?"

"It's the truth, ain't it?"

"*It's*...well, damn it, we don't know as yet. Provided no abscess forms in the wound, I'd say he has as good a chance as any."

"And that's an educated assessment with you being a horse-thief and all instead of a doctor?"

Bill stood up fast, his bloodied hands balling into fists. "I don't see you stepping over here to tie a tourniquet."

"Never said I wouldn't."

Bill held out a hand, gesturing an invitation. "Then would you be so kind as to put your ass into motion and hold him while I push the bone back in?"

Frank put his hat on and spit into the dirt. "Don't mind if I do."

Bill and Frank worked quickly, but the screams still came. By the time the bone had been set, Jimmy was whimpering like a beaten dog, the stick between his teeth nearly chewed to splinters. There wasn't much else that could be done for him. They gave him room to lie in the dirt and left him to his tears.

Frank went off to fetch a canteen. When he came back, Sam Merton was limping beside him with two pairs of saddlebags and a coiled rope over his shoulder.

"Look who I found beating a dead horse," Frank said.

Sam let out an exhausted laugh. "I did no such thing. Only kicked him on account of my bags being stuck under him. Sonofabitch was heavy."

"How's your leg?" Gordon asked.

"Still attached. Ankle's twisted though. Much as I hate to say it, if our friendly lawmen up there happen to make their way down, don't think I'm gonna be doing much running."

Jimmy sat up fast, his voice gripped with fear. "You don't think they're coming down here, do you?"

Sam slipped his saddlebags off his shoulder and let them drop into the dirt. "Haven't seen them dangling down the cliff by a rope yet. And I'm starting to get the feeling that's the only way down at present."

Gordon looked out across the dry flatland toward a grove of trees lying in a deep hollow. Beyond that, perhaps a quarter-mile further, was another face of sheer rock, rising up to the desert plateau above.

They were at the bottom of a box canyon, he was almost certain, and not a particularly large one at that. But if the posse who had chased them down here was still committed to apprehending them, it would take some time to find another way down, maybe enough time for them to come up with a plan.

"You see any trails?" Gordon asked.

"Some worn ruts in the dirt," Sam said. "Nothing that looks like it's been used in years though. You thinking we can walk out?"

"Do you think we have any other choice?"

"From what I can see? No. But with my ankle being as it is, I'd prefer riding to walking. I don't suppose any of the horses are still alive?"

Bill Webb shot an irritated glance at him. "You see one standing here, sniffing the dirt? I thought you Tennessee boys were supposed to be sharp."

Sam lifted his left leg and gripped it below the knee with both hands, pulling it toward his chest to stretch it. "You know me, Bill. I'm as dull as a doorknob. But I figured I'd ask anyway."

Bill slapped his hands on his trousers, wiping off the blood. "We're walking out or we're climbing out. And after that, it's still a good twenty miles to Branchwater. And twenty miles when we're walking wounded might as well be a hundred. Of course we have you to thank for that."

Sam's eyebrows went up. "*Me?* How the hell do you figure that?"

"You were riding out ahead of the rest of us. And I didn't hear you ask for our opinion when you tugged on the reigns and turned onto the trail that led us down here."

"Hey, you didn't have to follow me either! But at the time, I didn't see us having much in the way of a choice, unless we wanted to end up like poor Tom. You gonna stand there and tell me you would have done something different? Or were you comfortable with the idea of riding over open country and taking the risk of having a bullet drill into your back?"

Bill shrugged. "It's no worse than getting nearly killed in a rockslide. No worse than getting trapped at the bottom of a canyon with no way out either. And being trapped down here with you is just about the worst thing I can imagine."

Sam charged forward, moving surprisingly quick despite his twisted ankle. "Listen, you rotten-mouthed bastard –"

Gordon stepped between them just as the fists began to fly. On any other day, he'd let them have at it. Their tempers had flared more times than he could count. And a black eye or swollen knuckles wasn't uncommon for either of them. But down here, after what they'd already been through, he couldn't allow it.

"*Stop it*," he said. "*You just cut it out and save it for another time.* Before you two kill each other, let's talk about how we're gonna get out of here."

Sam unclenched his fists and nodded toward the hollow behind them. "I know I'm not too sharp and all, but trees mean water. So there's a creek or river back there. We crossed one up at the top, remember? Chances are, it runs all the way through. Chances are we can follow it."

Gordon smiled, feeling optimistic for the first time since they'd gotten here. "Yeah, we might try that. Maybe it leads to –"

"Shit!" Bill said, his eyes widening.

He dropped into a crouch, making himself small behind a negligible mound of dirt.

"*What?*" Gordon asked. "*What is it?*"

"There," Bill said, pointing over the treetops towards the other side of the canyon. "There's someone up there with a rifle."

Gordon felt his heart jump. He started to move, to seek out cover where there was none, his eyes darting back and forth between the dusty ground and the wall of rock beyond the hollow.

Then Frank was beside him, grabbing him by the arm, and pushing him down into a depression barely large enough to fit a coyote. The big man took cover beside him, pulling the rifle from his back.

"Where is he?" Frank yelled.

Bill pointed, trying to keep his head low. "In a tree. Near the top. Saw a flash."

Gordon squinted, searching the face of the cliff, moving from crag to crag. Three-quarters of the way up, he saw it – a flash coming from a small pine clinging to the rocks, the unmistakable glint of sunlight reflecting off the barrel of a rifle.

"You think he's seen us?" Gordon asked.

"If he hasn't, he will," Bill said. "Got a view of the whole canyon from up there. We're no good here. We've gotta get to better cover. We should make for those trees."

Gordon lifted his head slightly, his heart hammering against his sternum. He looked in every direction, at the piles of fallen rock and the broken bodies of the horses, at the men crouched around him, at the place high up where the flash had come from.

He turned to Frank. "Help the kid."

They ran and limped and staggered over open ground, moving at a speed that felt deathly slow, stumbling and picking themselves back up, their feet sliding through the hardpan and sending thick clouds of choking dust rising into the air around them. It invaded Gordon's nostrils, carrying the smell of burning, cut only by the scent of his own sweat, and, more faintly, the blood from Jimmy's wound.

He was half-blind now, chasing the silhouettes ahead of him.

The seconds passed, and the fear grew.

A bullet was going to find him.

He knew it as a fact.

He could see it in his mind as clearly as he'd seen Tom go over the edge of the cliff.

He would fall right here, and they'd leave him in the dirt to rot.

Then it was over.

They stood in a grove with branches over their heads, surrounded by mesquite and scrub oak and Arizona pine, breathing hard and taking stock of themselves. There was good cover here. Gordon could barely see the wall of the canyon through the small gaps in the canopy.

But he still didn't feel safe.

It was Bill Webb who found the cave.

He'd gone wandering off, searching down by the banks of the narrow river, where the trees leaned over the water to offer shade from the merciless sun. A quarter mile east, he came to a spot where the wall of the canyon curved inward, forming a natural overhang that kissed up against the grove beside the shore.

When Gordon saw it for himself, he was felt an overwhelming sense of familiarity. As if he had been here before.

It was in the shape of the rocks and the twisting of the roots in the sandy soil, the way the river bent in a lazy curve, and the waters slowed to almost mirror stillness, reflecting the sky above and memory now ten years distant.

In the summer of '79, he had come west to the territory to make his fortune in silver. He and Tom Talbert had staked a claim in a remote canyon, far from the boom in the open country where the prospectors were cheating and killing each other for prime land. They had spent two months living off of canned beans and rabbit meat, sweating out long days beneath an overhang of red rock, churning up tons of earth and finding nothing. As summer turned to fall, they'd turned their attentions to other pursuits, riding out into the prairie to rustle cattle and keeping them corralled in the canyon for a week or two while a drunken horse doctor from Saskatchewan used a hot iron to change the brands.

But this was not his canyon.

He could see that clearly.

This canyon had belonged to someone else, and they had come and gone some time ago, leaving behind the things they'd used, or broken and made useless. They lay strewn across the ground outside the entrance to the cave, half-buried in the dirt, skeletons in a mercantile graveyard. Here a rusted can. There a shattered lantern. A circle of stones arranged into a fire pit. A boot with no sole. A belt buckle. An empty wooden crate with the word "explosives" stenciled across it.

The cave had once been a silver mine. And from the looks of it, little more than an impressive failure, a dark tunnel bored and blasted into the rock and shored up with roughly hewn beams of thick timber. Gordon wasn't sure how deep it went, but he'd have wagered ten dollars that no man had been here in a decade or more. It belonged to the rats now, and they'd scattered their fetid droppings everywhere. But until they found a way out of the canyon, it would have to serve as shelter.

As the low afternoon sun cast long shadows, they built a fire, setting it far back from the mouth of the cave to hide its light from the canyon walls above. Soon, the evening grew cold and they huddled close to the flames to ward off the growing chill, the rich scent of mesquite smoke cutting through the foul air. In the distance, the steady slosh of the river seemed to become quieter, its sound replaced by the steadier crackling of the burning branches and, more faintly, the scurrying of rats in the darker depths.

Gordon sat silently, listening to the men as they spoke of how they might leave this place, planning, musing, proposing hypotheticals. But only Sam and Bill gave it much attention, somehow finding a way to turn it into another argument, placing blame on each other for their current predicament. Jimmy Jones sat shivering with his knees pulled up to his chest, paying little attention to rest of them, denying himself the room they'd given him to move closer to the fire. Sitting further away, Frank seemed content to rest his broad shoulders against the wall of rock and sip a brown bottle of Laudanum.

Despite his desire to remedy the situation and have a constructive discussion about their plans, Gordon's heart wasn't in it. He was too tired, too weighed down by the thought of what had happened to Tom. Every time he brought himself to the verge of speaking, his mind turned to the fall, the feeling of the ground disappearing beneath him, being swallowed by the dust and smothered.

After a time, Jimmy let out a small cry and pressed the fingers of his good hand into his cheeks. He stared at Frank, watching the bottle glitter in the firelight.

"Let me have some of that."

Frank eased the bottle from his lips. "Only got the one. And it came from *my* saddlebags."

Jimmy's face contorted in desperation. "Come on, Frank. Just let me have a little. My arm is broke for God's sake."

Frank looked at him, impassive. "And my ribs are broke. I'm not inclined to share." He took in the others sitting around the fire, judging, resenting, scorning them. "And if any of you try to take it, I'll bust your heads."

Jimmy lowered his eyes, trembling.

Gordon turned to look at the big man sitting behind him. "Let the kid have some, Frank. He's smaller than you. He doesn't need much."

Bill laughed, tossing a stick into the fire. "Old Frank needs more than you think. He's the only man I've seen drink patent medicine the way some men drink whiskey."

Frank lifted the bottle and took another sip. "This is better than whiskey."

"And it's precisely what the kid needs right now," Gordon said.

Frank gritted his teeth. "I said —"

"And now *I'm* saying. Give it to him."

An unspoken threat passed between them. Gordon had known Frank a long time. He knew what Frank could do to him, just as he knew that Frank would never actually do it.

Frank glared, seething with bitterness, and then conceded with a nod. He stood up and handed the bottle to Jimmy. The kid sipped slowly and let the opium still his suffering.

Gordon turned to the fire, watching until it burned low and sleep overtook him.

Morning brought warmth and pain.

Gordon could feel it everywhere. In his head. In his chest. In every joint and limb. It throbbed and stabbed, punishing him with each guarded movement. It wasn't until he stood and stretched and ran his fingers over the tense muscles that he was able to convince himself nothing was broken.

The pain was there, and it wasn't.

Perhaps it was another kind of pain.

In his mind, or in his soul.

The others awoke and grumbled, stricken with real injuries. Frank was opium-dazed and off-balance, walking around in circles in search of his boots. When he found them, he grunted in disgust and tossed them back into the dirt, sending something small scurrying out of the collar on multiple legs.

"Goddamn, scorpions!" he said. "May they perish from the Earth."

"Maybe they just like you," Bill said, grinning.

"Maybe you should shut your mouth and see about making us some breakfast."

Gordon fed twigs to the smoldering ashes of the fire and brought it back to life, filling the already warm cave with an almost unbearable heat. They cooked salt pork and beans, and ate eagerly. All of them except for Jimmy. He lied curled up, beside the fire, his eyes wide open, unseeing. They tried to rouse him, but he was somewhere else, caught between consciousness and sleep.

After they finished eating, Sam limped to the mouth of the cave and stepped into the soft morning light. Gordon followed him to the water's edge.

Minutes passed, and neither of them spoke. For the first time, they truly noticed it. There was beauty in this place, a quiet perfection they had long ago forgotten how to see. Before now it had seemed as if there had never been time. Time was money. Time was work. Time was days hunched over ledgers in musty offices, or digging fence posts while the foreman cursed and demanded expedience, or scheming up ways to make a living that didn't involve bosses. Time was nights shivering in tents in railroad camps, or sweating at the poker tables in search of good fortune, or lying beside a woman who could offer warmth but couldn't calm the doubt and the fear and the voices that questioned the things that were supposed to be certain.

Gordon felt it all around him, the harmony of a world barely blemished by man, all things existing in balance.

But as he looked at his feet, the illusion was broken.

There he saw a keg of kerosene, slowly rotting and leaching its oil into the water, forming a swirling multi-colored film across the surface.

A thought occurred to him then, and he spoke it: "Are we bad men?"

Sam shuffled in the sand, turning to face him. "What makes you say that?"

Gordon lifted his shoulders, as if it was an answer, and then added: "It's something I think about from time to time."

"Maybe you think too much."

"I might."

They fell into silence again. A minute slipped past.

Sam spoke, his voice full of indignation: "We're not badder than anyone else. No...we're...we're not even that bad. We're only doing what we have to do, aren't we?"

"I suppose we are."

"And we've never killed anyone in the pursuit of that. Not in the pursuit of scratching out a profitable vocation. I killed men during the war, sure. But that was war. War is different."

"I know that. I mean, that's what I've heard. I don't know it the way you know it."

Sam stared out across the river, his eyes becoming far away. "You'd be surprised what you can live with. And the things you can't, you change. And believe me, a man *can* change. When the war ended, I told myself I had to. I told myself I was done with killing, and I've stood by that.

"I know you were too young to fight, Gordon. So, you don't know what it was like. What it was like after. When it was over, I was so full of hate I thought it would destroy me. I wanted to kill. I needed to.

Everywhere I looked, I found someone deserving. I found a reason to do it.

"My daddy had himself a farm in Sullivan County. Small place. Sixty acres. But you should have seen it. It was like Heaven on Earth to me. He worked that land for twenty years. Tilled the soil with own two hands. Sweated over it day after day.

"Then the bank came and told him he needed to pay up. And he didn't have the money. He couldn't get a line of credit. Couldn't rightly borrow it either when everyone else was trying to put the pieces together. The war had up-ended everything.

"He held out as long as he could, but it didn't make any difference. This...*Carpetbagger*....from Boston came along and bought the farm direct from the bank. He just showed up at my daddy's door one day with the signed papers and told him to get out. Didn't give a damn that he had nowhere to go. He wanted him out right then and there, or he'd have him locked up for trespassing on private property.

"Can you believe that? A man works half his life at something, and has it taken away like it's nothing.

"When I heard what happened, I knew what I had to do. I knew that I was gonna find that Carpetbagger. And I was gonna kill him. Even if I'd hang for it.

"But the day arrived when I meant to do it, and something came over me. There was this aching in my guts. I felt sick. I thought about killing him, and the more I thought about killing him, the sicker I felt.

"It was like a poison flowing through me.

"I wanted to kill him, and I knew I couldn't. I couldn't kill anyone ever again.

"And every day, I remind myself of that. I tell myself that I've atoned and changed. I'm not like some of those folks who make the papers. You're not like that either. I wouldn't even carry a gun if it wasn't an occupational hazard. But other things we do...that doesn't hurt anyone. Not really."

Gordon touched the holster at his hip, allowing his fingers to brush the steel of the pistol there. "We just scare people a little."

"That's right. We play the role of the badder men because that's what gets the result we need. You saw how it was with that stage. The driver believed we were prepared to kill. And sometimes belief is stronger than anything. It doesn't matter if you fire a shot or not. If a man believes the shot will come, he'll cower and do things he wouldn't do under normal circumstances. And he sure as shit will hand over the money, or anything else you care to take from him."

"But the things we take...people always want them back."

Sam leaned against a tree and lifted his foot to stretch the bad ankle. "You still think they're coming after us?"

"I don't know. They were awfully eager yesterday."

"They were that. Maybe we got lucky though. If you can call it luck. Maybe that fella we saw up there didn't see us, and they figure we died in the fall. Maybe he's gone by now."

"Maybe. But maybe he's still up there. And I don't think we should decide anything until we know for sure. If we have to, we could stay down here for a few days, stretch out the food we've got. Stay out of sight and see if they're willing to come down and get us."

"I can get behind that mule. Doesn't mean it'll plow for Frank or Bill though."

"You let me talk to Frank. I can reason with him. And steer clear of Bill. You two are a bad pair."

Sam cracked half-a-smile. "Now, Gordon, you know I'm a civilized man at heart. While Bill and I have had our...*differences of opinion*...I'm amenable to the idea of peaceful coexistence. Of course, when I was a younger man, I would have gladly stuck a bayonet through his Yankee hide, but he'd have done the same to me, so all's fair."

Gordon laughed, and looked out across the river toward the far end of the canyon. The morning sun was beginning to burn brightly along the top of the red rock. Despite the growing warmth, it would be a few hours before it washed over the canyon floor. It wouldn't reach the cave until at least midday.

A thought came to him then, fully formed and already on his lips before he gave it any more consideration.

"Do you still have that pair of field glasses?"

"Yeah. In my saddlebags. But they got smashed up in the fall."

"How bad?"

"Didn't take much time to look, why?"

"I need them. Get Frank, too. Tell him to bring his rifle."

He couldn't see, but he was confident that he couldn't be seen either.

Gordon sat in the shaded bow of a mesquite tree with Sam's field glasses in his hands. They were exactly as Sam had said – smashed – but not entirely useless either. One barrel had been crushed and flattened, the lens completely destroyed. The other was merely cracked.

He placed it to his eye and carefully adjusted the focus. He saw the damaged glass, blurred and amorphous, growing brighter and then darker as he slowly panned from left to right. He stopped to wipe the lens with his shirt, and tried again.

"Can you see anything?" Sam asked, his voice hushed to a whisper.

"Not yet."

Frank shuffled his feet impatiently. "I don't see why we're wasting the day on this."

"Just wait," Gordon said.

He aimed the field glasses at a narrow gap in the leaves and squinted. The image was still a mess, too abstract to be recognized. He slowly adjusted the focus, took a moment to judge the increase or decrease in clarity, and then adjusted some more.

Slowly, the blur took on shape, the non-color deepening to red and brown and orange.

He saw the canyon wall, pocked with fissures and crevices, ribbed with folds like the skin on the back of an old train conductor's neck. He tilted upward, passing over jagged ledges and crags. There were shrubs and saplings growing on narrow overhangs, defying wind and gravity.

Further up he saw a tree, a gnarled pine with its feeble roots knotted over the rocky mantle, its twisted branches out-stretched in contrition.

He saw the man sitting in it.

He was little more than a dark silhouette, barely large enough to fill the eyepiece. He sat on a branch, riding it the way a man would ride a horse. His arms held something, ill-defined and long. The field glasses were too damaged to make it out clearly. But he knew it was a rifle.

Gordon handed the field glasses to Sam and climbed down.

"He's still there."

"Alone?" Sam asked.

"Looks that way."

Frank stepped closer to the tree and looked up through the branches at the distant wall of the canyon. "The rest of them could be camped out up top. Maybe even provisioned for a week or more. One thing's for sure, he's got a view of the whole canyon from up there."

"But he has to know where to look," Sam said. "What's to say we can't sneak out after dark? He'd need eyes like an owl to see us then."

"Or ten other sets of eyes with pairs of glasses up at the top of that cliff helping him out. Which he may have. But as to the matter of walking out, that would depend on there *being* a way out."

"There's a river right there. River's don't go nowhere, stupid."

"And last I heard, a man can't walk on water unless his name is Jesus Christ. Let's say the other end of this canyon narrows to ten feet with rock all the way up and fast-moving water below. You know how to swim, Sam?"

"Yes, I know how to swim, *Frank.* And we don't know what's at the other end of this canyon. So, why don't you postpone your bleak assumptions for the time being?"

Frank spit into the dirt. "I could do that."

"Situation is, he's up there, we're down here. And we all know why that is."

"Why is that?" Frank asked. "Because we had the dumb luck of getting caught in a rockslide? Or because we were dumb enough to trust Charvet when he said taking that parcel would be an easy job?"

Sam thought about it for a moment. "Both I guess. But Charvet never did wrong by us before."

"There's always a first time."

Sam leaned closer, looking worried. "You think he...*turned us in?*"

Frank shook his head and nodded up toward the cliff. "That fella up there? He's like...rain in the middle of the dry season. There's no good reason why you should think it'll rain. But sometimes it just does. Without warning. Without any prior indication. I think Charvet is the sort who would write for the Farmer's Almanac. I think maybe he believes he's got a keen sense of these things. It didn't rain in July for ten years in a row. So he's confident that come July next year, it won't rain either. Then July rolls around, and it pours. We're just the poor saps who happened to get caught in it."

Sam stepped back, shaking his head, walking around the stump of a splintered, lightning-struck cottonwood, sub-consciously avoiding the patches of light that shined down through the canopy onto the dry leaves. "Dumb luck or not, I'm not gonna just stand around and wait for them to come to me. I need to be doing *something* about this."

"Never said we shouldn't. I just err on the side being realistic."

"Then let's be realistic," Sam said, his voice wavering. "Let's find a way out of here. Let's go back to Branchwater, send a telegram to Charvet, give him his parcel, get our money, and forget this ever happened."

He stopped walking around the stump and took a seat, nearly falling as his ankle gave way. He sighed and muttered to himself, and ran a hand through his graying hair. Gordon thought Sam looked too tired for a man his age. The war and a hard life in the desert had added twenty years to him, turning him into an old man at forty.

Gordon's mind took a sudden turn inward, viewing himself through the same lens. He wondered if it was happening to him. He was a younger man by ten years, but for ten years he had lived the same kind of life, a life that could slowly wear away the best of a man.

He quickly dismissed the idea, writing it off as a side effect of fatigue from the growing heat and a night of broken sleep.

He looked up at the cliff, considering the matter at hand once more, and then turned to Frank. "If you had to, could you hit that tree with a shot from your Sharps?"

"Hit the tree? Maybe. Hit *him* on the other hand? I highly doubt that."

"You wouldn't need to hit him. I just need to know if you can get close."

"I can't be sure. If I was on the other side of that river, and found a good spot with some elevation, there wouldn't be any question. But from here? I might as well be throwing rocks."

"If you fired a few shots at him though, would he know where you're shooting from?"

"I wouldn't fire more than one or two shots at him for that very reason. And who knows what he has up there. Probably a goddamn buffalo gun with some kind of magnifier strong enough for him to see a flea on a gopher's ass at a thousand yards."

"But if he does have something like that, he's not gonna be looking out over every inch of this canyon. He's gonna be looking at one tree, trying to find the one man taking a shot at him."

Sam lifted his head, looking hopeful. "We could distract him. Son of a bitch. That could actually *work*. He'd be looking down the wrong side of the canyon while the rest of us slip out."

Frank frowned and picked up his rifle. "It still means one of us would have to stay and take a few shots. And I'm not volunteering."

"I'm not asking you to," Gordon said. "But I wouldn't ask you or anyone else to stay behind either. A few shots is all we'd need. Then we all walk out. Together."

"*If* there's a way to walk out," Frank said. "If."

The sun wasn't with them.

At the cave, there was talk of scouting the far end of the canyon to the west for a way out. But as the morning wore on, the protective pall of blue shadow cast by the high eastern cliffs was quickly drawn back from the canyon floor, revealing the river and the trees to the world above.

None of them dared to venture out into the sunshine unless he was safely beneath cover. And even then, there was still reluctance. There were places where the branches had been torn away, gaps where entire trees had fallen or never grown at all. There was no way to travel from one end of the canyon to the other. Not without walking out in the open. Not when the sun was up.

As the last of the shadow crawled back into the rocks an hour before mid-day, Bill and Gordon walked east along the wall beyond the canyon, following the river. What they found there was a dead end. The walls on either side of the canyon drew together into a horseshoe, holding a waterfall within its grasp. At the bottom it tumbled and crashed over rocks and boulders, raging as rapids for two hundred yards before it calmed and fed the grove.

At noon, the sun touched the entrance of the cave, and they sat, tired, in the shade, talking little and eating a meal of dried meat. Gordon could feel the pain again, everywhere and nowhere, growing and shrinking, breathing through him. He thought about Tom Talbert and hated himself for thinking. He hated that in this place, all a man *could* do was think, to wait out the heat of the day, impatient for the promise of something unseen.

He pretended to be interested in last week's newspaper, reading articles that meant nothing to him. A train had derailed and killed 80 people in Ireland. The British were fighting the Mahdists in the Sudan. Marxists were holding an international congress of workers in Paris. Sullivan had gone 75 rounds with Kilrain in a ring in Mississippi and won. A prominent New York industrialist was denying rumors of blackmail and infidelity.

When the news of the real world proved impossible to focus on, he tried reading the latest installment of William Edward Tanner's serialized novel, *The Moon Kingdom*. He'd been following Captain Percival Arrington's adventures for weeks, waiting to see if he could successfully slash his way through the fearsome armies of King Shangh, and rescue Princess Allura from his evil lunar clutches.

But this too couldn't help him escape.

There were only the thoughts and the pain that came with them.

He blamed himself for what had happened to Tom.

Tom hadn't wanted this life.

Tom had gotten out.

In the fall of '79, when their cattle rustling had begun to draw too much attention, he had boarded a train and gone back east. It was nothing personal. Even when their claim had turned up little more than dirt, those days had been the best of their lives. Swimming in the small creek that trickled through the bottom of the canyon where they had made their home. Lying out beneath the stars beside a well-tended fire and talking late, off-loading the burden that every man was expected to carry in silence. They had found something better than what they had gone looking for. Every summer had to end, but their summer had been perfect.

After Tom left, he had moved around a lot, working respectable jobs that didn't pay respectably, never living in one place for more than a few months. But they had never lost touch.

In '84, he had married a woman in Chicago. Gordon hadn't really understood it, but he had taken a train east to see them down the aisle. Tom was a changed man by then. He had drifted away from the life he'd had out west and traded it all for a badge and uniform. He was happy, he said. He was ready to settle down.

Then the bomb had been thrown in Haymarket Square in the spring of '86, and seven officers had been blown to pieces. Tom had gotten scared. He had gone looking for a quiet life. He thought he'd found it. And now there were riots in the streets, and people were dying. It was changing him in ways he didn't want to change. It was one thing to fear death, and it was another to fear being asked to beat a man because he was raising his voice for better pay and better conditions and encouraging his fellow workers to strike.

Gordon had encouraged him to come out west again, to live on his own terms, to bring his young wife with him and make a home here. Tom was reluctant, but he gave in halfway. He would move out west, but he wouldn't bring his wife with him. He couldn't let her see what it took to make a living out in the territory any more than he could let her see what kind of man her husband would become back in Illinois.

He took to carrying a cheap gold pocket watch with her portrait inside the cover, a reminder that he was still a loyal partner. He sent her letters and money, and made promises of returning home soon. But "soon" was stretched out for three years.

Gordon had always given him reasons to stay. There was always another job or opportunity. They had become acquainted with Charvet and done steady work for him, taking the things that his anonymous clients wanted them to take.

It wasn't a good life, but it was a living.

Until Tom had died.

Gordon stood, feeling the pain flow and then ebb. The heat was suffocating him.

He dropped the newspaper and walked deeper into the cave, allowing the darkness to envelop him. He sat against a beam, breathing the foul stench of the rats, listening to their scratching movements.

He waited.

Waited.

Waited.

Hours later, he heard the arguing, the voices filled with accusations bleeding into each other. He pulled himself up from the cool ground and walked toward the light, watching the silhouettes of Bill and Sam stab the air with pointing fingers.

"Lower your damn voices," he said. "They can hear you all the way back in Branchwater."

Bill and Sam fell silent, their raised hands foundering and then dropping to their sides.

Gordon stepped between them. "Now, one at a time, tell me what all the hubbub is about."

Sam went first: "We're almost out of food. Only got what was in my saddlebags, and that wasn't much. I figured since the sun is going down and all that maybe, under cover of darkness, we might try retrieving the other saddlebags. But Frank says he isn't carrying anything we can eat, aside from dope, and Bill says he doesn't have any food. Jimmy ain't said a word all day, so who knows what he's got. And I didn't figure you were carrying much either, Gordon. So, I suggested, quite innocently that maybe we should eat one of the horses."

"That wasn't the way you put it," Bill said. "You tell it to him like you told me."

"I didn't *tell* it any other way."

"Yes, you did! You know you did."

"All I said was –"

"All you said was I should go out there and get killed!"

"Stop it," Gordon said. "We're not doing this again!"

Bill tried to push past him. "You can't fool me, Reb. If you want me dead, you're gonna have to do it yourself."

Gordon pushed him back. "I said *stop!*"

Bill stumbled and caught himself, bracing an arm against the wall of the cave to keep from falling over. As he regained his balance, he curled his hands into fists. He took a step forward, looking at Gordon, wanting to hit him. Within a second, he realized what he was doing and stopped himself.

"Hey, Gord. I'm...I'm sorry. I don't know what got into me. It's just that he –"

"I'm sure he's thinking the same about you, Bill. But I don't want to hear any more of it unless you're gonna keep it well mannered. Do you understand?"

"Well, yeah."

He turned to Sam. "How about you? Do I have to explain it again?"

Sam held up his hands in surrender. "No, sir. I understand completely."

Gordon stepped back, testing the tentative truce he'd just brokered by giving them enough room to start swinging. They eyed each other, considering it, but didn't make a move.

"Now tell me," Gordon said, "without pointing fingers, without raising voices, what the situation with the food is."

Sam walked over to his saddlebags and pulled out a paper sack. Gordon could hear the stray bits of jerky rattling inside before Sam opened it and showed him how little there was.

"Is that all?" he asked.

"That and a piece of salt pork. Hardly enough for one man, let alone five."

"What was this about eating one of the horses?"

"Well, I figured, one of us could go out there and maybe cut off a leg. Only been out there a day. The meat should still be good enough to eat after we put it on the fire."

"He was volunteering *me* to do it," Bill said.

"I was *asking* you. Because you used to be a butcher."

"Yeah. Damn near thirty years ago, when I was younger than the kid. Doesn't mean I wanna go running out there when some Johnny Sureshot is sitting up top with a rifle. And I sure as shit don't appreciate you volunteering me for it."

"I'm sorry, I just thought…"

"Yeah, you just *thought.* Thinking never was your strong suit, Sam."

Sam frowned. "What's that supposed to mean?"

"It means I never could understand how a Tennessee man could fight for the Confederacy. Unless he's got no brains between his ears."

Sam stepped forward, his hand dropping to the butt of his pistol. Gordon reached out and grabbed him by the wrist, squeezing tight.

"*Don't.*"

Sam looked at him, his eyes filled with violence.

"When we get out of here," Gordon said, "you two can do whatever you want. But right here, right now, I need you to be calm and courteous. If you kill each other, it's just gonna make it harder for the rest of us. And I don't have a shovel, so you'd forfeit a Christian burial."

Bill grinned. "You could forego a burial altogether and serve us up as a Donner Party dinner."

"We'd give you a mighty bad case of indigestion though," Sam said.

"Sam, you and Bill already do," Gordon said.

Sam and Bill laughed, friendly again, or at least pretending to be friendly. He would have to watch them closely.

This place was bringing out the worst in them.

As the sun dipped beneath the plateau to the west, they built another fire.

Even without enough food for a full meal, they placed the pan over the flames and cooked the single strip of salt pork, cutting it into five equal pieces. As they ate, they tried in vain to make conversation, but the words faded and drifted off, bled dry of enthusiasm.

Frank produced the bottle of Laudanum, now half-empty, and turned it over in his hands, looking at the flames through the brown glass. He pulled the stopper, and tilted his head back.

"How are your ribs?" Bill asked.

"They're not cooking on the fire, waiting to be served for sustenance." He lifted the bottle in a toast. "This fine libation helps quell the appetite though."

"I don't suppose you'd be willing to save some of that libation for the rest of us just in case it's needed."

"You suppose correctly. Besides, the kid hasn't said a word all day."

Bill slid away from the fire and turned to Jimmy. He sat clutching a canteen, huddled in a small alcove worn into the rock. The flickering light of the flames drew shadows in the hollows of his pale, thin face.

"How are you feeling, Jimmy?"

Jimmy drummed his fingers on the canteen, saying nothing.

"Kid, are you feeling sick?"

Jimmy's gaze shifted upward, taking in Bill and the rest of them sitting around the fire.

"I've got this terrible thirst."

"Drink some water, kid. You've got some in hand."

Jimmy shook his head, his eyes losing focus. "There's nothing in it. Hasn't been all day."

"You haven't had water all day?"

"Water won't be enough. I never had a thirst like this before. It's...it's like the whole inside of me is empty. Like I could drink the whole world and I'd still be parched."

Bill stood up and walked over, kneeling to look at him more closely. "Kid, when was the last time you had something to drink?"

"I can't remember."

Bill placed a hand on his forehead. "You're burning up."

"We're all gonna burn."

"For Christ's sake, Jimmy. Don't talk like that. Gordon? Frank? Somebody wanna go down to the water and fill his canteen?"

Jimmy closed his eyes and pulled away, hugging the inside of the alcove. "No. That water's dirty. I'm not drinking it. I'll catch my death."

Sam got to his feet, wobbling on the bad ankle. "That water's safe, kid. Been drinking it myself all day. I'll get you some."

"No, not you. Not anyone. You're gonna poison me. You're just waiting for me to turn my back."

"That's not what we're doing," Bill said. "We're trying to help you."

"You're not!"

"*We are*. Listen to me. You know us. You've known us damn near two years. You're not feeling yourself. Which is to be expected when your arm is broke and you don't drink for a day."

Jimmy shook his head, over and over, crying now. He reached out and grabbed onto Bill, collapsing against him.

"I'm being punished, that's what it is."

"Punished? What are you talking about? Punished for what?"

"For the things I've done. I've done awful things. Things I've never even told."

Jimmy buried his face in Bill's shoulder. The older man hesitated and then wrapped his arms around him, gently placing a hand on his back.

He spoke softly. "You just hush up about that now. You're a good kid."

"I'm not. I'm *not*. There was this...this boy...lived in the same town as me. Went to the same church. His mother and mine were friendly. They thought we should be friendly, too. But I never liked him. I...I *hated* him. Didn't even have a reason. I just hated him. Hated seeing him every day. Hated hearing him speak. Hated having him follow me everywhere I went because his mother told him he was my friend.

"One day...one day I was up on the hill outside of town. No one was around but me and him. He was...talking to me...laughing...saying things. I wasn't even listening. I just looked at him and I wanted him to stop. So, I *pushed* him. I pushed him and he fell. He fell like we fell. He went down the hill, and when he got to bottom, he was dead.

"They didn't find him 'til the next day. I said I hadn't seen him. I lied to everyone. I went to his service and said a prayer with his mother. And the whole time I was thinking about how I killed him. And I didn't feel a thing. I wondered how it was even possible to not feel something. Like there was this...big hole in the middle of me. And it's been there ever since."

The tears flowed.

Bill held him.

The rest of them watched, not knowing what to say.

"I've done awful things, too," Bill said. "Terrible things. But there's nothing we can do about it now. Why don't you get some sleep? I'll get you some water."

Jimmy pulled away. "No...I don't want to be a burden."

"You're not a burden, kid. You're one of us. And we look after our own."

"I still don't want you treating me like a child. I'm a grown-up man. I can get my own water. I *will* get it."

Jimmy got to his feet awkwardly, the sling around his broken arm causing it to stick out an odd angle like a broken wing.

"Are sure you're okay?" Bill asked.

"I'm dandy."

"Why don't you let me get the water?"

"No. I'll get it. I got one good arm."

Jimmy walked toward the mouth of the cave, moving quickly. Bill trailed close behind.

"Don't mother him," Frank said.

Bill stood in the opening, half-bathed in moonlight, watching as the kid walked down to the shore and knelt at the water's edge. "I'm just making sure he's safe. That's all."

Frank walked over and clapped a hand on his shoulder, pulling him firmly until he took two steps back into the cave. "You can make sure he's safe from in here, Bill. He wants to be a man, let him."

"Hey, I'm letting him get it himself, aren't I?"

"I can't drink this," Jimmy called out. "It's got oil in it."

"Hold on a second," Bill said. "I'll come give you a hand."

Frank laughed. "So, you're letting him get it himself then."

"I'll just show him where to get it. That's all."

"Oh, for Christ's sake," Sam said, pushing himself up. "Enough of this dilly-dallying." He limped to the mouth of the cave, and leaned against a beam to take the strain off his ankle. "Kid, just walk out a little ways. It's fresh as well water. No mud or anything."

"Are you sure?"

"You want me to get it? How about Bill? You got plenty of grown men ready to fetch it for you."

"I'll get it. *Leave me alone.*"

Frank shook his head, chuckling. "That boy is stubborn."

"You're a shade stubborn yourself," Bill said.

"Yeah, but age has refined me into the gentleman you see before you."

"What a bunch of horse shit."

"You being a horse thief, you would know a lot about that."

They all heard the scream.

Gordon saw it first, his heart shuddering as he looked beyond the fire and out of the cave, seeing Jimmy thrashing in the water a few yards from shore, being pulled away on the current.

He was on his feet and running within a second. By the time Bill and Frank turned and saw what he saw, he was nearly out of the cave. And then all four of them were hurrying outside together, skittering over dirt and rock toward the river. Bill moved out ahead, galloping into the water in a full sprint that quickly slowed to a jog as the river rose above his knees. He charged forward and the water climbed to his hips, to his waist, to his stomach. He battled against it, refusing to give up.

And then he stopped, realizing exactly where he was standing, the treetops ending and the sky opening up above him.

"Sweet Jesus," he said. "Swim, kid! Swim!"

Jimmy was already fifty feet out, his head just above the water, his good arm flailing. He kicked and thrashed, barely keeping himself afloat. He cried out, begging for help, from them or perhaps from God Himself. His voice echoed off the distant rocks, becoming smaller, carrying broken prayers that distorted as the waves lapped over his face and replaced the air in his throat.

Frank ran through the grove, moving faster than any of them could hope to match, trying to keep pace with the kid and still failing. Gordon tried to follow, slowing as Bill struggled to reach the shore, half-swimming/half-running through the water. Gordon stepped closer to help him, reaching out a hand.

Bill yelled: "Don't stop. Go get the kid."

Gordon did as he was told, and Bill staggering up the embankment, his strength completely sapped. Sam limped toward him, finally catching up. They nearly collided, and Bill stumbled past him, shouting.

"Get the rope, goddamn it! It's the only chance he's got!"

Sam muttered an unheard reply and pivoted on his good ankle, running back toward the cave in uneven strides.

Bill hurried down the shore, trying in vain to reach the kid as the current pulled him away, shouting for him to swim even though he knew damn well that Jimmy couldn't.

Gordon was closer now, but he could already see the water that far out was moving faster than a man could run, pulling the kid further and further away until his cries faded in the vastness of the canyon and his face became silhouetted in the distance. He saw the arm move back and forth, splashing, the dark head bobbing up and down, disappearing beneath the rushing sheet of silver and then coming up again, the panicked voice cutting in and out, over and over, until the head went under one last time and the voice fell silent.

When Bill returned to the cave, something about him had changed.

As he set himself down beside the fire, he didn't say a word. He stared into the flames, his eyes lost, his body slumped and thin like a newborn foal.

The silence smothered them all, overtaking the sound of the water and the crackling of the fire.

Bill kept staring.

Staring.

In time, he looked up and blinked.

"Why didn't you bring the rope?"

Sam lifted his head. "Bill, I'm sorry about Jimmy..."

Bill's voice was flat: "The rope. Why didn't you bring it?"

"I...I *did*. You were far down the shore by the time I could get it. And Jimmy...the water was too fast. You know that. We all saw it."

Bill looked at him, through him, the light of the fire and pure hatred burning in his eyes. "You killed that boy."

Sam's mouth fell open, wordless for a moment as a lump in his throat moved. "What are you saying that for? I didn't do a thing to him."

"You told him to go walking in the water. You didn't bring the rope."

"Now hold on. You *hold* on. I told you, I did. I can't much run with my ankle twisted, but I brought it fast as I could. And I can't be blamed for the kid walking out too far. He was sick. You saw he wasn't right. I offered to fill his canteen. He wanted to do it on his own."

Bill's lips pulled back from his teeth, sneering as he spoke: "It should have been *you*."

Sam's jaw clenched. "If you were so concerned with that boy, why didn't you jump in and grab him then? You can swim."

Bill hesitated, the anger conflicting with the undeniable truth that the rest of them knew.

"You know why," he said. "You *know* why I couldn't go out there."

Sam frowned, looking disappointed. "And yet you blame *me?* You blame a cripple for being crippled, when you were but fifty feet from him. And all you had to do was swim to him and pull him ashore. Seems to me, if you had done that, he'd be sitting here right now, drying himself by the fire. Instead of dead."

Bill's eyes filled with tears. "I couldn't. You know I couldn't! You know he's up there. He could've shot the kid if he wanted, and if I'd have swam further out, he could have shot me, too! We step out in the open and that's how it'll be. He's got us all trapped and there's not a damn thing we can do about it!"

Gordon put a hand on his shoulder.

He spoke softly. "That's enough now. Let's get some sleep. Tomorrow we'll try to find a way out of here."

Bill wiped his eyes and nodded.

They all lied before the fire in an imitation of slumber, their heads cushioned by folded arms, their eyes closed. Gordon pretended like the rest of them, but sleep didn't come. His mind wouldn't cease thinking. He saw Jimmy in the water, thrashing and screaming. He saw Tom falling from his horse, a look in his eyes like he'd seen death carrying away everything he held dear.

The thoughts drifted into waking nightmares. He saw the canyon, but it was different somehow. Contorted forms that vaguely resembled men emerged from the shadows, as if they had been waiting there all along. They climbed down the cliffs and the trunks of the trees and crawled through the grove, their long arms reaching out with midnight claws, holding the darkness of a world beyond the known world. They converged on the cave, slithering inward, wrapping themselves around the fire and snuffing it out. Their forms changed then, the absence of light allowing them to become what they truly were. They expanded like fog and settled over their sleeping pray, allowing themselves to be breathed in.

Gordon opened his eyes with a start, hitting his head against the wall of the cave. He looked over and saw the fire still burning. He saw the men sleeping around it, or at least pretending to.

He sat up and rubbed his face, and then stood.

He couldn't breathe in here.

He was boiling.

He walked out into the moonlight, and moved through the grove, stripping off his clothes and draping them from branches until he was completely naked, letting the night air cool him. He found the stump of the lightning-struck tree and sat down and looked through the small gaps in the leaves, up at the canyon wall and the pine rooted to the rocks near the top.

He wondered why.

Why some men lived and others died.

All these years, he hadn't given it much thought. But he knew some men deserved to die more than others.

Tom Talbert was the least deserving man he'd ever known.

Tom had been good.

Even in the midst of their awful business, he had taken the gold watch out of his pocket from time to time. He had opened the cover to reveal the small portrait inside, and gazed at the woman who was waiting for him back in Chicago. Every time he had done it, Gordon had caught a look in his eye, one he had seen for a brief period ten years ago, but was now reserved for someone else. The look of a man in love.

Gordon gazed up at the distant tree and wondered if the man sitting in it felt anything at all.

In the hour before dawn, they walked the length of the canyon.

A strong wind had picked up, howling over the rocks and dropping downward, tugging at the branches in a steady wave of movement, rising and falling and then rising again. It was the first bit of luck they'd had in two days. The entire canyon floor was awake and writhing, the sight of it too much for one pair of eyes above (or even a dozen) to focus on.

They followed the river west, moving from tree to tree, running across the small patches of meadow where the grove was open to the charcoal sky.

It wasn't a long walk. A mile at most. And when they reached the end, they saw what Frank had always known.

The walls narrowed, terminating in a slot less than ten feet wide. It forced the river into a bottleneck, roiling the water into a chaotic spray of foam that dragged roughly over the red sandstone. A man would have to be out of his mind to try swimming it. Even going with the current, he'd last a few seconds at most. And then time would stop with the breaking of his bones.

As the faint light of morning brightened in the eastern sky, they returned to the cave, defeated, walking as a funeral procession, in mourning for the ones they had lost among them, and the ones they were still yet to lose.

Day rose without ceremony, bringing heat and sweat and imprisonment once again. The food was gone. They starved quietly, basking in the shadows, taking care not to move more than they had to.

By mid-day, the madness was setting in, driving away all reason and replacing it with panicked fever. Sam cursed himself and stood and limped to his saddlebags, muttering about traps and snares, the tricks he'd learned as a boy back in Tennessee. He could catch a rabbit or a squirrel in the grove, or even one of the rats at the back of the cave. He could bait it with crumbs. It wouldn't be much, but they'd be able to eat almost everything on the carcass, even the marrow in the bones.

Off he went into the shimmering air, becoming a near-mirage. When he returned an hour later, he was drenched in sweat and hunched over, his fingers blistered.

"Is he still there?" Gordon asked.

Sam's voice was a dry croak: "I didn't look."

Deep down, Gordon knew he didn't have to go and check.

But the urge was too strong to resist.

He needed to see for himself.

As he stood in the grove, looking through the field glasses, he saw exactly what he had imagined he'd see, what he'd dreamed about as he sat slumped over in the shadows, caught in a half-sleep.

The man was still there in his tree, mocking them with his patience.

Gordon hated him, wishing that by some miracle the rocks above would come tumbling down and crush him, knowing bitterly that it wouldn't happen.

Day after day, the man would remain there. Waiting for them to perish.

They sat in their cave, willing night to come and give them some small fraction of comfort.

When the sun finally set, Sam went out to check the traps.

He looked sullen when he came back.

"Maybe you were you right," Bill said. "Maybe we should eat one of those horses."

"Who's going out to get the meat?" Sam asked. "You?"

"Me and someone else. I'm not going alone."

"I'll do it," Gordon said. "Let's get this over with."

"It's not right," Bill said, his voice becoming dangerously loud in the dark. *"It can't be."*

They stood at the base of the moonlit scree, walking parallel to the cliff, their eyes tracing the slope of broken rocks and finding nothing.

"It can't be. It's not possible."

Gordon shushed him, dropping into a crouch and motioning for Bill to do the same. He pointed up at the scar cut into the rock high above them, his finger hovering over the gaping black mouth that had been a mere grin two days ago.

"Another rock slide," he whispered. "It must have fallen away when the wind was up. The horses could be six feet down."

Bill looked at the scar for a long time, needing to convince himself. "But why didn't we hear it?"

Gordon shook his head. "I don't know. The way the wind was howling? Someone could have taken a shot at us and we'd have never heard it."

Bill's eyes drifted over Gordon's shoulder to the other side of the canyon, trying to find the tree.

"You think he's watching us, don't you?" Gordon said.

Bill nodded, his hands clenching and unclenching in front of him.

Gordon reached down and picked up and a jagged shard of rock, no larger than a silver dollar. He squeezed it in his hands until he felt pain, and then let it drop.

The fear was still there, but somehow it was different, almost comforting now, a kind of strength he could draw from. He wouldn't run. He wouldn't show weakness. He would sit and wait, regardless of the outcome.

"Maybe he is watching us," he said. "Maybe he's thinking it over carefully, deciding if he's gonna pull that trigger. Maybe he doesn't want us to go so easy. Maybe he wants us to starve instead."

"We *are* gonna starve."

"Not if we leave."

"And how are we gonna do that, Gordon? You saw what we all saw. There's no way out."

"No way to *walk* out. So, if we can't walk, we'll climb. You, me, maybe Frank. I don't know if Sam would be up to it with his ankle, but if he wants to try, we let him try. And if he doesn't, we'll still do what we can for him. We'll go to Branchwater, get some fresh horses, and then come back for him."

Bill looked down at his feet, using the toe of his boot to nudge the rock Gordon had dropped. "I don't know. I just don't know anymore. If you'd asked me yesterday, I'd have been scrambling up that rock faster than any other man. But now...I feel so tired. After seeing Jimmy...I don't know if I have anything left."

Gordon reached out and gripped his shoulder. Bill looked up, surprised.

"*Listen*. I know it's bad. Worse than that even. But if we don't try to get out in the next day or two, I don't think we ever will. You know I'm right. And you know you can make that climb if you have to."

Bill sighed. "I suppose I could. Yeah. But what about...what about *him?*"

"I think he expects us to try. And if we tried climbing up right here, chances are we wouldn't make it. He'd get a shot off before we could reach the top. So, we'll climb up on the other side."

"But how? If we try to cross that river we'll —"

"It's gotta be easier than we think. You saw how it was just a ways down from the falls. There are a lot of rocks, maybe enough for a man to get across. And once we're across we go straight up under him. It's the one place he won't be looking. And when we get up there, you know what we have to do. We have to end him. If we don't, it'll be us. So, I'm asking you. Are you with me or not?"

A minute past as Bill considered it. Finally, he gestured an unenthusiastic "yes" with a single nod.

"We go tonight then."

"What? Now?"

"Maybe an hour or two. Long enough to talk it out with the others and fill our canteens."

Bill's head dropped. He ran his hands over the back of his neck, trying to knead out the tension.

"I can't do it. I can't. Not tonight."

"You can."

Bill looked up, his face pale and withered in the harsh moonlight.

"I've barely slept a wink in two days. If I could just...just sleep one night. A little sleep. I can do it if I sleep."

"Bill, if we wait another day, without food..."

"Sam will trap something. You'll see. We won't *really* starve. I didn't mean it. We'll be all right for another day. One more day to sleep and regain my strength."

Gordon started to speak, ready to protest, and then hesitated.

He could see the exhaustion, the utter destruction that had befallen his friend in a matter of a few hours. It had eaten away at all of them in different ways, large and small, since they got here, but he understood now that Bill was the worst. For all his uninjured physicality, his mind was broken, the will to go on almost completely shattered.

He felt sympathy trickle and then flow within him, washing away the voice of reason that told him he should go himself, to climb out tonight on his own and leave this blighted place far behind. The voice that replaced it whispered something else, a lie that would bring temporary comfort at best.

"Yeah," he said. "Yeah. You're right. It's better if we go tomorrow. Sam'll get us a fat, juicy rabbit. Maybe even a couple of them. We'll have a big dinner before we make the climb."

If sleep had come, Gordon wasn't aware of it.

He spent the night in a middling place within his own mind, trapped between memory and tired oblivion. When he rose from the hard ground at first light, Bill was stooped before the fire with a handful of sticks, tending it.

Gordon didn't ask if he had slept.

He already knew the answer.

Without a word, he walked out into the grove and found his place among the trees, climbing to the bow some seven feet off the ground, now worn-free of bark by the friction of denim and fingernails. He sat and stared through the field glasses, watching the man in his own tree on the other side of the river.

The hours past, the heat of the day growing along with the thirst in his belly. But still he watched, never looking away, ignoring every ache and instinct to sustain himself. The man was toying with him, testing his patience by proving he could sit longer, denying his own need for food and drink, refusing to even move one hand to unfasten his pants and relieve himself. He was a statue, swayed only by the breeze and the weight of his weapon, tugging at him just enough to catch the sun and cause a flash.

Gordon watched and understood that this was madness.

This was the end of all reason.

To sit and wait and see oneself fade away without a care or regret, dedicated to the task and nothing more.

As the sun set, he returned to the cave, stopping at the shore to kneel and drink until his guts were seized by a cramp. The others had built a fire, but only Frank sat close. Bill was tucked into the rocky alcove that had belonged to Jimmy, sleeping or pretending to sleep. Sam sat propped against the opposite wall, staring intently at a box wrapped in twine and brown paper sitting at his feet. A few seconds passed before Gordon realized it was the parcel they'd taken from the coach three days ago.

Gordon sat, wiping the drops from his chin. "What's with him?"

"He's been like that all day," Frank said. "Except for about ten minutes when he went to check the traps."

"He catch anything?"

"You smell food cooking on this fire?"

Gordon thought of his hunger, distant and well-buried. Weakness hadn't yet afflicted him, but it waited just as the man waited in his tree. Patient and prepared to bring an end to him.

He pushed the thought away and forced himself to smile, feigning good humor. "I must have lost my sense of smell in the fall."

"You must have lost your sense, too," Frank said. "Staying out in the heat all day. Thought you might have died out there."

"If you'd have really thought that, you'd have gone looking."

Frank lifted a heavy chunk of dry wood and dropped it on the fire, sending a swarm of embers flying. "Only because you still owe me five dollars. I can't rightly leave a debt unpaid. Even if a man is on the verge of the great beyond."

Gordon reached into his pocket and fished out a handful of coins. He tossed them at Frank's feet.

"You're paid in full."

Frank reached down and scooped them up, holding them in his palm reflecting the firelight for a moment before closing his callused fingers around them.

"Much obliged, Gordon. You decide to wander off again, I'll let you die in peace without rummaging through your britches for legal tender. Speaking of which, where did you wander off to?"

"You know where."

"Don't see why you waste the time."

"There's a lot of time around here to waste. And besides, someone should be watching."

"Anything new to watch?"

Gordon shook his head. "Same as it was before."

Frank slipped his hand into his pocket to deposit the coins. When he pulled it out again, he was holding the bottle of Laudanum. He set it on his knee, letting it slosh. It was mostly empty now – two inches of bitter liquid sitting at the bottom. He pulled the stopper and tilted his head back, gulping until there was only an inch left.

He sucked his lips dry, savoring every last drop, and set down the bottle. He pulled off his boots and slid his stocking feet close to the fire.

"Bill says you and him are climbing out tonight."

"Me and him and anyone else who wants to try."

"I might. Ribs hardly hurt at all."

"Medicine will do that. Might loosen your grip, too, if you have too much."

Frank wrinkled his chin in a non-expression that was too displeased to be a smile and too amused to be a frown. He raised the bottle, holding it lightly by the neck between his thumb and forefinger, twirling it around for a moment before taking another gulp.

He exhaled in exaggerated satisfaction. "My apologies for imbibing. Sometimes I need a bit of loosening."

Gordon saw the dull intoxication in Frank's eyes, disguised by years of practice. Soon he would be nearly useless, a man walking through thick mud, sinking deeper and deeper with every step.

He wouldn't bother to argue.

Instead, he turned and looked at Sam. His eyes were still fixed on the parcel, the way a predator looks at its prey.

"Sam, are you all right?"

Sam didn't answer.

"Sam?"

"No point in trying to rouse him," a voice said.

Gordon turned and looked at Bill. His eyes were half-open now.

"Wouldn't speak to me or Frank either," he said. "I called him a yellow-bellied turncoat and he didn't even twitch. Think he's lost his mind."

Gordon walked over and sat beside Sam. He reached out to touch him and then thought better of it.

"Sam, is there a reason why you're so interested in that thing?"

Sam nodded, continuing to stare, unblinking.

"Can you tell me what that reason is?"

"It's so plain," he said.

Gordon glanced at the parcel. It didn't look particularly special. Just a box like any other, the sort of thing that was shipped across the country and delivered every day. When they'd held up the coach, it had taken a couple minutes to find the right one because they all looked so similar, the only distinguishing feature being a New York City address.

"Are you worried Charvet won't pay us?" he asked.

"He'll pay. He always pays."

"What is it then? Besides the way it looks, I mean."

Sam was quiet for a long time. He still didn't blink.

Then he came to life again, leaning back slightly and flaring his nostrils.

"I never thought such a thing could be so much trouble."

"What do you mean?"

Sam allowed his eyes to leave the parcel, shifting them to Gordon to acknowledge him. Gordon saw the solemn determination there, the look of a man who knows something the rest of the world refuses to believe.

"It's the reason we're here, isn't it? If we hadn't been hired to steal that thing, none of this would have happened. Tom would be alive. Jimmy would be, too. It would be the same as it always was."

Gordon leaned over to touch the parcel, meaning to turn it to look at the address again. Sam reached out fast and grabbed his wrist, starling him.

"I have an idea," he said. "It's been in my mind all day. Tried to convince myself to forget it, but I can't. I think we should open it and see what's inside."

"*Are you off your rocker?* What's in there is no business of ours. We don't get paid to go nosing around what we take."

"Charvet never said we couldn't."

"But he expects us not to. If we open it, chances are he won't pay."

Sam smiled. "I don't much care anymore. I *need* to know."

Gordon looked to Frank for support, and then Bill. Neither of them protested. They were all too tired to make an issue of it.

"Fine," Gordon said, throwing his hands up. "If you want to explain to Charvet why it was opened, you go right ahead."

He turned away, putting his back to him as if it would convince him to leave the parcel be. He listened as Sam lifted it, unknotting the twine, and tearing away the paper, removing a lid and lifting the contents within.

"Son of a bitch..."

Gordon looked over his shoulder. Sam was holding something flat and rectangular. It flexed and warped in his hands, reflecting the light of the fire, projecting a yellow spot onto Sam's face.

"Goddamn...carpetbagging...son of a bitch!"

Gordon leaned closer and saw that it was a photographic print, a sharp image of a naked man and woman in the middle of a very private act. If he had only bothered to look for a second, it would have meant nothing to him. He would have mistaken it for the sort of illicit art one could find in shops that catered to a very curious variety of customer. But he gave it enough time to know better, to allow his eyes to study the faces and recognize them.

The name didn't immediately come to mind, but he knew the man's reputation. He knew how much money the man had and that his fortune was growing by the day, built on steel and coal and railroads and land he'd snatched up cheap in the days after the war when business-minded Northerners had swept into the South looking for new financial opportunities. He knew the woman in the image wasn't his wife, though much like his wife, this woman was young and beautiful. He knew the man got whatever he wanted because men like him always did, and even though he had much to lose, he was smart enough to avert a scandal and the inevitable divorce it would bring by hiring an unscrupulous sort of man like Charvet to hire more unscrupulous men to steal the damning evidence before it could fall into the wrong hands.

Sam pulled himself up from the ground, bracing his arm against the wall to compensate for his ankle. He walked over to the fire and dropped in the photograph.

Gordon shouted: "Wait!"

He crawled toward the fire, trying to reach it in time.

Frank was closer, but he did nothing. He stared at the flames in a Laudanum daze as the photograph caught fire. Bill was on his feet, trying to do something, reaching down to grab it and pulling his hand back in pain. It was too late. He could only stand and watch as the paper browned and curled, the man and woman in their lustful act turning into a fine sheet of glowing ash before crumbling.

"Why in God's name did you do that?" Bill asked.

Sam shrugged, his eyes still focused on the fire. "All Carpetbaggers should burn."

Bill clasped his hands together tightly, rubbing the singed fingers. "Oh, here we go again. Let's hear *all* about how your daddy couldn't pay the bank and a big bad Northerner swooped in and bought the farm out from under him."

Sam stepped back from the fire, the anger on his face becoming more direct, focused solely on Bill. "You have no cause to talk about my kin like that."

"Which way is that, Sam? I'm only repeating the story you've told a hundred goddamn times. But how about you include the part where your daddy drank half his money away, and lost the other half playing cards? Or better yet, how about you tell us where *you* were when all this happened? Oh wait. We've heard that one, too. We've heard it a hundred damn times because you never shut up about it. You were all broke up when the war ended and didn't have two pennies to rub together, so you went to West Virginia and took to stealing coal wagons. And how about this? How about you tell us what any of that has to do with that damn picture? Is that hen-pecker the same fella who bought your daddy's farm?"

Sam opened his mouth to speak, hesitated, and then started again. "Well, no. He's not the *same* one. But I know the type."

"Oh, you know the type. You know a thieving Northerner when you see one."

"Yeah, I do."

"And you hate them more than you hate anything."

"Yes!"

"So, since you hate them *so damn much*, why don't you tell me why you burned the damn picture? You probably just did the man a favor."

Sam's hands clenched into fists. "I wasn't doing him any favors."

"Oh, how is that? I mean, *objectively speaking*, how does destroying it hurt him in *any* way? You know who he is. You've read the papers. You've seen what he's caught up in. Doesn't take much to figure out that we were stealing the damn picture for him. And why do think he'd want it? So he could put it on the front page of one his publications? So he can announce to the whole world that he's pecking a hen that isn't bound to him in holy and legal matrimony?"

The fists waved, shoulders squaring as Sam's voice rose in volume: "I don't care what he wants. I don't work for thieving Northerners."

Bill's voice was calm: "You *don't?* You just burned the picture. You saved him the trouble of having to do it himself. Hell, he doesn't even have to pay Charvet now. Which means Charvet doesn't pay us. Which means he's such an astute thieving Northerner that he figured out a way to get a proud Tennessean who hates his guts to work for him for free."

Sam limped forward, the fists aiming in a new direction. "I told you, I don't work for him! If I'd have known who hired Charvet, I wouldn't have touched it. And I'll tell you something else, when I get out of here, I'll go to New York and cut his goddamn Yankee throat myself."

"Oh, now we're on to the Yankee talk again. Let's hear all about the war and the things you saw and the things you did, all those Yankees you killed in battle, and how after twenty-five years you haven't moved on like the rest of us."

"Are you telling me what I can or can't feel about it?"

"No. I wouldn't presume to tell you anything. The wax in your ears is so thick, you wouldn't be able to hear it if I was screaming it in your face. But since it seems like I have your attention, I'd like to remind you that the war is over and *your side lost.*"

The anger burned brighter than the fire, but Sam moved slowly, limping closer to Bill, his raised fists prepared to strike.

His voice wavered, unsteady. "I killed men like you in battle. If I'd seen standing there on that field, weapon in hand or no weapon, I'd have spilled your blood and washed myself in it."

"Big talk," Bill said. "Sometimes I think you weren't even in battle. You probably tried to enlist and they figured you were too slow in the head. Probably had you running a stretcher and carrying the corpses of more capable men."

Sam swung, but it was Bill who landed the first blow. The punch grazed Sam's jaw and ricocheted over his shoulder, the force of it pulling Bill against him. They grappled each other, their legs moving together in a tangle as their weight teetered back and forth. Bill pushed at him, trying to break his grasp, growling and cursing.

After a moment, he was free, standing there, out of breath, looking at Sam as Sam looked back at him.

Gordon could see it on their faces, what they both intended to do.

He ran toward them, shouting: "Stop!"

Sam lunged fast, reaching for Bill's throat.

He wasn't fast enough.

Bill drew his pistol and fired.

The shot thundered off the walls of the cave, torturing their ears and leaving behind a sharp ringing.

Sam stumbled back, grabbing his stomach. The blood seeped between his fingers, staining his white knuckles. He fell to his knees, letting out a pained groan.

Bill lowered the gun, breathing hard. He looked satisfied and disappointed at the same time.

Sam's mouth hung open, showing a twisted row of yellowed teeth. He clenched them, shaking his head, and reached for his holster.

The second shot was quieter, almost dull. Bill turned his head and looked down at Sam and then at the hole in the middle of himself. He leaned back against the wall of the cave, trying to keep on his feet, and then slid into the alcove where Jimmy had made his last confession.

Sam laughed, but there was no humor in it. It quickly turned into a cough and then a pained moan. He flopped forward, reaching out to break his fall, and crumbling under his own weight. He lied there, his head turned to look at the fire.

"Goddamn Carpetbagger," he muttered.

Gordon saw the life leave his eyes, his lips moving wordlessly and then becoming still as a thin line of blood trickled from the corner of his mouth.

Bill tried to sit up and slumped down again. His legs sliding across the ground until they were splayed in front of him. He looked at the palms of his upturned hands lying useless in his lap, and then cried in silence, as if he felt a deep shame more than he felt the pain of the bullet.

And then he was gone.

Frank got to his feet, stepped back, and bumped into the wall next to Gordon, trying to put distance between himself and the horror he saw before him. He lifted the bottle with a trembling hand and took a gulp, losing half of it down his chin.

"This goddamn place is cursed," he whispered. "He's killing us and he hasn't even lifted a finger."

Gordon placed a hand on his shoulder. "Frank...somehow we have to..."

Frank reeled, his eyes half-deranged. "I'm gonna kill that bastard if it's the last thing I do!"

Gordon searched his mind for the right words, for a way to bring him calm and comfort. But there were none. Frank was driven now, a whipped bull charging at its enemy.

He dropped the bottle onto the ground with a hollow *plunk*, and took up his rifle from its resting place against a timber beam.

The only word that came to Gordon's lips was "wait." He repeated it, again and again, nearly shouting it as Frank stormed out of the cave and ran into the grove. Gordon gave chase, but Frank was faster, driven by an unseen force that no man had a right to harness.

As Gordon came within sight of the lightning-struck tree, he heard the first shot. His eyes searched, moving from trunk to trunk until he found Frank standing with the rifle to his shoulder, aiming up at the cliff.

He chambered another round within a second and fired again, not bothering to steady himself. Gordon ran, unable to cross the ground fast enough to stop a third shot and then a fourth.

Frank was screaming, sending every foul word he knew to the top of the canyon, and punctuating it with a bullet.

As Gordon reached him, Frank swung around, aiming the smoking rifle barrel directly at his face.

"*Stop*," he said. "*Please.*"

Frank gritted his teeth. "I've got him scared now."

Gordon felt the panic clawing at his chest.

"Don't you understand what you've just done?"

Gordon moved faster than he thought possible, running through the grove with Frank lumbering behind, having only half-understood the things he tried to tell him.

When they reached the cave, Gordon quickly gathered every bit of firewood he could find along the shore, piling it into Frank's arms and ordering him to bring it inside.

There was little time, but Gordon wasn't sure how much exactly. If he was right, it could happen any minute now. And if they weren't prepared, they were both dead men.

He tossed the branches on the fire, building it up so high that the flames nearly reached the ceiling.

Frank moved slowly, obeying his commands without questioning them, carrying Sam's saddlebags and the rifle into the dark, until they were forty feet from the flames.

When Gordon was satisfied that the fire would burn for a long while without needing more wood tossed on, he ran into deeper into and dropped onto his stomach behind a saddlebag, using it to prop up Frank's rifle.

Frank sat behind him, leaning on an elbow.

They waited.

Gordon wasn't certain what he expected.

One man or ten.

But he knew they were coming, and the shots were the last straw. They'd scale the cliff and cross the river and come for them, or maybe they truly were what he'd seen in his nightmares and they'd rise out of the darkness.

Maybe they'd known where to look all along.

And soon they would step through the mouth of the cave, the silver light of the full moon framing their tall silhouettes, their bodies remaining little more than walking shadows as they approached the fire, the glare of it dimly illuminating their featureless faces.

Time stretched, playing tricks. A minute was an hour. An hour was a day.

Gordon gripped the rifle tightly in his hands until his fingers ached. He stared down the sight and focused on the rising conflagration, prepared to shoot whoever stood behind it.

"I'm real sorry," Frank whispered. "I don't know what got into me."

"Don't talk."

"It'll be all right. I might have got him. He might not come after us."

"Frank, it's fine. Just keep your voice down."

Frank shivered, and lifted the bottle, pouring the last of it down his throat. In the dark, his dope-sick eyes were nearly black, completely lost.

"But even if he does, we can outsmart him. He thinks he's got us trapped, but he doesn't."

"Frank, we *are* trapped."

Frank shook his head, and crawled backwards a couple feet, waving his hand toward the far end of the tunnel.

"Don't you see, Gordon? The way out has always been down. We can go deeper. Deeper than any other man has ever gone. We can live inside the Earth, Gordon. You and me and the rats. We'll fool them all. We can stay down here forever. It'll be like in those fairy tales. Trolls and goblins. We'll rule them like Kings. They'll treat us like Gods. We don't need daylight. *We don't need the sun.*"

"Shut up! Shut you goddamn stoned mouth, Frank! Or I'll oblige you and bury you down here."

Frank stared at him, confused and oblivious, but he didn't say a word.

Gordon turned his attention back to the rifle and the mouth of the cave beyond, trying to block out everything else, including his own thoughts and the monstrous fear that stoked the fires of his locomotive heart.

He was only a man and the thing of his nightmares was also a man.

A bullet could put an end to him.

One shot and it could all be over.

He waited, dedicated to the task as the hours passed.

But no one showed.

Somehow the sun still rose.

Gordon lifted himself up from the hard ground, breathing the thin smoke from the smoldering fire, and walking to the mouth of the cave to watch the sky brighten. Behind him, Frank stirred, rolling over and coughing as he threw a thick arm over his eyes, muttering a curse at the encroaching daylight.

He was lucky to have slept at all. Gordon would have happily traded places with him for a few hours of peaceful oblivion.

The urge to step back into darkness and rest was almost unbearable, but he willed himself to stay on his feet, driven by a fathomless determination.

He would see this through.

He would find a way out.

He paced back and forth in the mouth of the cave, waiting for Frank to rouse himself, his hand occasionally dropping to the ironwood grip of the pistol firmly secured in the well-oiled holster at his hip. Until now, he'd had little cause to use it. It was akin to a prop in a stage production. Something to intimidate coach drivers and night watchmen. Loaded only because there was always a slight chance that he might have to fire it.

All these years, he hadn't been prepared for that. Every job. Every detestable act of robbery. He had known that if things went sideways and descended into violence, he wouldn't be able to pull the trigger.

But he was prepared now.

He had been prepared last night. Thought last night he had been afraid. Today, it would be different. Today, he would show no fear. Instead, he would give in to the forbidding spirit he had spent years trying to avoid, the red animal that drove men to run across open fields of battle, rage-filled and hungry for each other's blood.

Gordon paced and imagined and impelled his mind onward, and then his eyes fell to the cave floor, moving over the lifeless bodies of Sam and Bill.

He felt his knees go soft, all that strength faltering as he reached out to brace himself against the wall.

Frank coughed again and dragged his feet through the dirt, kicking the empty bottle of Laudanum and sending it clattering against the rocks.

"Goddamn it. Shit."

Gordon walked deeper into the cave. "I take it you're awake then."

"Yeah, I'm awake."

"Are you sober?"

"Wish I wasn't."

"Do you remember last night?"

"Wish I didn't."

"I think we should bury Sam and Bill before it gets too hot. Then we should check on those traps and fill our canteens. And when the sun goes down, I think we should climb up that cliff and kill that son of a bitch."

Frank got to his feet, looking surprised and hopeful. "Man alive. When we get back to Branchwater, I'm buying you a drink."

Gordon felt an abrupt flutter of longing, spurred by Frank's optimism. He could see Branchwater on a Friday night, the smoky streets crowded with copper miners eager to spend their wages, pushing rudely past lamplighters dressed in unseasonable wool coats, hurrying to the nearest whorehouse or saloon, laughing, fighting, drinking themselves broke. He'd always felt out of place there, a sheep among wolves. An imposter who nursed a single drink for an hour and laughed at jokes he didn't care for only to avoid embarrassment. But he would have given almost anything to be there again, to sit in the musty rooms that reeked of tobacco-spit, waiting for Charvet to walk through the door and greet him in broken English tinged with Cajun French.

Frank walked toward the mouth of the cave, upbeat and very much awake. He talked of old times, taking care not to mention Bill or Sam or Tom or Jimmy. He mused about plans and money and woman and cards. The hell of the last several days was pushed aside, as if it had never even happened. They would return home and it would be the same as it had always been. Better than that even.

He walked around the smoldering fire, looking for his boots, and then stooped to put them on, laughing at a joke that Gordon only half-understood.

"Come on," he said. "Let me see a smile on that face. First time all week, I'm feeling lucky."

He continued to laugh, straightening his legs out one at a time, his back cracking audibly. He slid a foot into the first boot and pulled it up to his shin.

The laughter stopped, replaced by a wordless shriek that sounded like a hiss of hot steam.

"*Sssssssssonofabitch!*"

He wrenched his foot out of the boot and tossed it away, his eyes widening as a half-crushed scorpion tumbled out, a single glistening drop of venom beading at the tip of its twitching stinger.

Frank rocked back and forth, clutching the foot in both hands and tearing off the sock to reveal a red puncture mark on the arch.

He looked up at Gordon, flashing a thin smile. "Guess I spoke too soon. This hurts something fierce." He grimaced, trying to laugh through the pain. "Guess I'm gonna be climbing on a sore foot. Do me a favor and step on that little shit."

Gordon lifted his boot to oblige, but he could already see that the scorpion was dead. Its movements were pure reflex.

He kicked it into the ashes of the fire and crouched to look at Frank's wound. The skin around the puncture mark was turning pink, beginning to swell, and pushing out a slowly creeping runnel of blood.

Frank shook his head. *"God...damn...that hurts.* Still...could be worse. Could've been...a rattlesnake. I hate...snakes."

He gritted his teeth against the pain, breathing deeply. The air made a sharp whistling sound in his throat, as if it was being sucked through a narrow reed.

Frank pounded a fist against his chest and tried to cough.

"Shit...I should've saved some...of that...bottle."

The foot slipped out of his grasp and flopped to the ground. He looked at Gordon, his eyes filled with worry now.

"Frank?"

Gordon touched his arm and felt his racing pulse beneath the skin. Frank pulled away, but the movement was sluggish. He started scratching at his neck.

"I'm all right. I've just got this...itch." He feigned a smile. "Haven't said that since I bedded the wrong whore."

He tried to laugh, but it was dead air in his throat. His eyes bulged with panic. His mouth opened, as if to speak, but he was completely silent for several seconds, the fear growing, until his chest finally rose and he sucked in a gulp of wind with a sharp wheeze.

He managed to get out a couple words, but Gordon couldn't tell if they were "oh, Jesus" or "no, please."

Frank stopped scratching, his arms unspooling beside him as he fell back into the dirt. He looked up at the ceiling, his large body ticking with small movements, a quivering lip, a spasming finger, eyes flitting from side to side.

Gordon leaned over him, his own heart pounding. He spoke in frantic bursts of energy, making empty reassurances, his hands moving tentatively over the clammy skin as it turned pale. The breaths became fewer and farther between, growing more shallow until they stopped altogether. The eyes moved back and forth, slowing down. The pale skin turned blue. Gordon held a canteen to his lips and watched as the water pooled in his open mouth and spilled over his cheeks. He made promises of returning to Branchwater and buying him a drink and a clean woman, of reliving the good times that had never been that good. The eyes looked past him, moving only slightly, seeing the cave, and then rolling back, seeing nothing.

Gordon decided he was damned.

As the day wore on, he couldn't get the thought of it out of his head. No matter how hard he tried, it was always there, a fact as indisputable as the sun always rising and always setting. It was there with him as he sat in the shadows and prayed to a God he had never really believed in. It was there as he lied prone on the shore and dipped his face beneath the water, trying to banish the heat from his aching head, and considering for a moment the idea of keeping it there and letting the river fill his lungs. It was there as he buried Frank and Bill and Sam.

He looked back on thirty years of life and knew he had brought this on himself.

It had begun long ago, before he'd even traveled west to the territory; before he'd quit college and (in the words of his father) "thrown his life away;" before he had reached a curious age and taken to standing in front of the windows of tailors' shops on that busy Ohio street back home, admiring the smartly-dressed young men inside when all his friends were gawking at socialites in satin gowns; before he'd even left the womb, perhaps, when the nature of his soul was still being written by an unseen hand.

His entire life and every moment in it was marked by damnation, and in every corner of his mind that he searched he couldn't find a single memory that wasn't tainted. Even that perfect summer, when he and Tom had left their studies behind and run off to make their fortune.

That summer had changed them. That summer and all its promise had only led him to years of loneliness.

All the things he'd said and felt in that other canyon, *his* canyon, had meant nothing.

Tom had gone away.

And when Tom had returned, things were different. Even when they were in the same room, standing face to face, there had been an immeasurable distance between them.

Gordon had resented it and told himself there was no resentment. He had looked for ways to keep Tom from going back home. He had hatched plans and looked to Charvet for jobs, always with the promise that it would lead to something better. Every job would be the last. Every job would earn them enough to quit and retire. He had lied to him, knowing there would always be another, that the payday wouldn't amount to much. He lied because the lie gave him hope. Another week. Another month. One more year. To wait it out on the slim chance that Tom would change somehow and become his old self again.

He knew it had been wrong. He felt little remorse for the crimes he'd committed and the things he'd stolen, but it was the lies he'd told that made him feel guilty. His conscience remained clean for almost every misdeed, but he couldn't forgive himself for deceiving a friend.

He had led Tom astray and poisoned him with the same vile curse that had haunted Gordon his entire life.

The curse of *wanting* what he couldn't have.

The curse that drove men to fateful ends.

And so many of them had been ended. The memories of them tormented him, countless moments, going back to the day his life had first intersected with theirs.

Frank in some backroom in Tucson, pummeling bare-knuckle fighters in an illicit boxing ring.

Bill in a barbershop south of Prescott, working as an unlicensed doctor, patching up bank robbers.

Sam in a stockyard, stealing cattle and doctoring the records to show they'd been slaughtered.

Jimmy in a saloon, waiting for the piano player to visit the outhouse and then sitting down, pounding out a barn-burning rendition of "Oh! Susanna," and pinching the tip jar when he finished.

And Tom.

Tom walking across the university quadrangle twelve years ago, wrapped up in a heavy overcoat even though it was early autumn and still quite warm, a furtive glance, a smile that hid entire worlds.

He'd have gladly tossed all the other memories into the fires of hell if he could only keep that one. He accepted that he was beyond redemption, but he wanted that moment to remain pure, to be a light in all this darkness.

But as the sun set, he knew there was nothing, no part of him that could be saved from the curse. The poison was everywhere and everywhere he went the poison would spread.

So be it.

He walked into the grove for the final time and pulled the weathered keg of kerosene out of the dirt. He carried it west, straining against the weight of it, and found the stump of the lightning struck tree.

As he spilled the oil over the ground, he thought of Sunday school, the words of the preacher warning him of burning lakes in the infernal regions below. He didn't think he could manage something on that scale, but even after years of slowly seeping into the river, the keg was nearly full, and he didn't spare a single tree trunk for a hundred yards. When it was empty, he breathed deep of the sharp fumes, savoring the moment, and took a box of matches from his pocket.

Gordon struck one and held it between his fingers, looking into its flame.

It was such a small thing.

And yet it would do so much.

He tossed it into the kerosene and watched the blue flames spread low over the ground, turning the dead leaves and grass to glowing embers, coiling around the roots of oaks and cottonwoods in orange snakes, climbing upward rapidly into the treetops, jumping from branch to branch until the entire grove was a burning umbrella.

He walked through the smoky air, past the cave, toward the falls. Just below the rapids, he found a place where the slick rocks were close enough together for a man to walk across.

The other side of the river was nearly identical, but here the slopes below the cliff crept closer to the water, rising in chalky knees and shoulders that divided the woodland into isolated thickets. As he walked, he stayed near the shore where the trees grew uninterrupted, bathed in the sickly blood-red light from the fire on the other side.

He searched, keeping his eyes trained upward. When he was certain he'd found the right spot, he walked toward the base of the cliff. As he neared it, he saw that it had no defined beginning. The slopes were dotted with boulders and outcroppings, places where the dirt had been eroded away to reveal the rock beneath, gradually becoming steeper until there was more rock than dirt and the trees and scrub brush disappeared completely.

Gordon steadily ascended, walking at first and then using his hands to brace himself against the incline, almost crawling. He pulled himself up onto a ledge, hugging it closely to maintain his balance as he got to his feet and ran his fingers over the sandstone in search of handholds.

The climb was almost unrelenting. From the ground, it had looked as if a man could move over the rocks like a ladder, the ledges evenly spaced like rungs. But standing on it, he saw that it was mostly a trick of the eye. The rock was crisscrossed with bands of light and dark, but neither signified a protrusion.

There were stretches where he held on with nothing more than his fingertips and the toes of his boots, fighting the burning in his muscles as he moved sideways in search of a better purchase. He had never known pain like this, the agony of pulling his weight another foot or another inch.

When he was fifty feet above the treetops, he looked down at the fire across the river. It had spread a long way beyond the kerosene, but it was starting to die out. It had served its purpose though. High above him, a pair of eyes would be watching, and if they watched the flames, they wouldn't be looking straight down.

He allowed himself a few minutes of rest, and then continued upward. The moon was out now, casting its pale light onto the cliff and revealing the handholds he'd have otherwise missed. It was a small bit of luck, but he refused to feel hopeful. He would need cold austerity to get through this.

He was aware of the open air behind him, its coolness seeping through his clothes, just as he was aware of what one wrong step would mean. He was aware that he was losing all sense of time again. Every inch was an eternity in a forever night, a torture that proved to be the one thing that could distract his mind from regret.

The feeling of loss should have overwhelmed him. It should have crippled him, or driven him insane. But it didn't. He kept climbing, pulling his weight higher and higher until his fingers were numb, his legs like lead. He looked up along the wall of the canyon and saw the tree. So close now. Forty feet. Thirty. Twenty. He willed himself to reach it, to see the face of the man who had held them here.

As he neared it, he forced himself to breathe slower, to become a whisper in the night air. He spidered his way over the rocks directly beneath it, looking up and seeing thick, gnarled roots clinging to the cracks. He saw a leg dangling, snakeskin boots, and blue jeans. Slowly now. Slowly. He moved sideways, his breath becoming ice in his throat, and pulled himself up along the other side of the tree. He saw both legs now, the edge of a shoulder illuminated in the moonlight.

Gordon reached high above him and gripped a narrow ledge, pulling himself up as he reached for his pistol with the other hand.

The man in the tree came fully into view.

For a moment, Gordon felt triumph. The man didn't move. He was unaware, vulnerable. Gordon drew his pistol and aimed, his heart thudding as he pulled back the hammer. He started to squeeze the trigger.

His finger froze.

The man wasn't sitting, although Gordon could see know how it had appeared that way from the bottom of the canyon. The gap of open space above the branch between his legs was no more than a few inches, and the sharp, broken sticks that dug into his shirt and suspended him there were all hidden behind his back, giving the illusion that he had been sitting. But up close, there was no mistaking the posture, the limp arms and legs and the head hanging forward, the long straight branch about the size of a rifle resting in his arms. There was no mistaking now that the man had fallen from a horse at the edge of the cliff above, and by some cruel twist of happenstance landed in the tree the way he had. There was no mistaking the gold pocket watch that hung from the man's vest on a long chain, slowly turning, the open cover flashing dimly in the moonlight just as it had flashed brightly in the sun. And, even though Gordon couldn't see it, there would be no mistaking the small portrait of the woman inside, waiting at home in Chicago for a dead husband.

Gordon lowered the gun and stood there on the ledge, gripping the rock with one hand, his body becoming heavy. He began to laugh, his voice dry and haggard, echoing in the emptiness. He laughed until his eyes filled with tears and he couldn't tell if it was laughter or crying.

He felt his fingers slipping on the rock and his toes loosely perched on the foothold, his body being pulled. He kept laughing, crying, throwing his head back and letting it pour out of him. He let it fill the night. Letting everyone and no one hear it. He felt his fingers slip free of the rock and his weight teetering, his toes taking all of it for a moment, and then his body swaying back, moving freely into empty space.

Falling back into the darkness of the canyon.

Dyer Wilk was born and raised in California, where he spent his formative years consuming a steady diet of movies, television, and paperback books. Eventually, his interests turned to writing and graphic design (for which he is most known). His horror and science fiction stories have appeared in several anthologies, and his illustrations and designs have graced dozens of book covers, including this one.